Ghost Rescue

AND THE
HORRIBLE HOUND

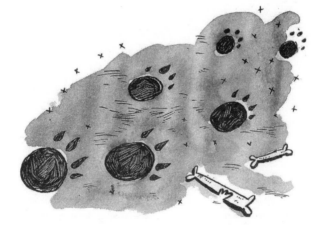

WRITTEN BY
Andrew Murray

ILLUSTRATED BY
Sarah Horne

ORCHARD BOOKS

ORCHARD BOOKS
338 Euston Road, London NW1 3BH
Orchard Books Australia
Level 17/207 Kent Street, Sydney, NSW 2000
First published in hardback in Great Britain in 2009 by Orchard Books
First published in paperback in 2010
ISBN 978 1 84616 354 8 (hardback)
ISBN 978 1 84616 362 3 (paperback)
Text © Andrew Murray 2009
Illustrations © Sarah Horne 2009
1 3 5 7 9 10 8 6 4 2 (hardback)
1 3 5 7 9 10 8 6 4 2 (paperback)
Printed in Great Britain
Orchard Books is a division of Hachette Children's Books,
an Hachette UK company.
www.hachette.co.uk

Charlie stared at the seven suns. They were on Yatterdee's right leg. Their colours had once been bright, when Yatterdee was alive. However, now he was a ghost, they were pale and silvery, with just the faintest memories of colours.

"They're great!" said Charlie. "Can I see the rest of you?"

When Yatterdee took off his glasses, his
eyes twinkled with kindness and fun. In
life, he had been a tattooist, and even as a
ghost, the faint ink stains of his job could
still be seen on his long, clever fingers.

He was covered in tattoos — Celtic knots and twining serpents on his arms, the seven suns on his leg, monkeys that seemed to hang onto his ribs, and on his back a great sailing ship surrounded by sharks and octopuses, walruses and sea-spiders.

Charlie and Ghost Rescue had just saved Yatterdee and his two ghost friends, Max and Mary. An evil fairground owner had forced them to work in his ghost train.

"Cool!" said Charlie, as Yatterdee showed him the tattoos on his back. "Can you still do them? As a ghost?"

"Well," said Yatterdee, "I've got my ghost-tattoo needle and ghost-tattoo inks...so I reckon I could do a *ghost* tattoo."

"A ghost tattoo? What's that?"

"A ghost tattoo is invisible to living people, Charlie, but visible to ghosts, or anyone looking through ghost glasses, like mine."

They were interrupted by the computer. *"Beep. You have email."*

Charlie and the Ghost Rescue team – the ghosts of Lord and Lady Fairfax, their daughter Florence, Zanzibar the dog and Rio the parrot – peered at the computer screen.

Dear Ghost Rescue,

My name is Monica Clancey. We have all just moved to a new house – Dad and Mum, me and our cat, Cookie. The house is next to a graveyard. As soon as we arrived, I felt there was something strange about the place. Cookie was spooked as well – he was hissing and spitting and fluffing up his tail at nothing – or so it seemed...

"That very first day I began to see things. A movement in the bushes. A shadow darting so quickly between the graves I couldn't be sure I'd seen anything.

"Then that night, as it grew dark, we heard a terrible howling. Dad said not to worry, that it was just a neighbour's dog — but it seemed so close. It sounded like it was coming from the graves…

"And then…! I'm shaking again, just thinking about it. I was asleep and something woke me. The night was quiet and moonlit, and for a moment I wondered what had disturbed me. Then I saw the eyes. Fiery red eyes, staring at me. I saw the shadow of a gigantic hound, standing at the foot of my bed. And then it growled…

It sounded like some great rumbling engine from hell. The room shook, and I think I screamed. With foaming jaws and great white fangs, it *leapt*…and passed straight through me, straight through the wall, out into the night.

Since then we have all been "attacked" by the hellhound. Now we are living in a shed at the end of the garden, as far from the graveyard as possible. We are all terrified. Please, Ghost Rescue, can you help us?

Monica Clancey

Charlie and the Ghost Rescue team
headed for the old pizza delivery van that
served as their Ghostmobile.

"Can I come too?" asked Yatterdee. "I'd
love to help, if I can."

"There's always room for one more ghost," smiled Charlie. And as well as the Fairfax stone, he put a piece of Yatterdee's headstone in his bag. Ghosts cannot move far from their stones, so Charlie had to carry them whenever he wanted the ghosts to go with him.

As usual, Charlie slid down in the driver's seat to work the pedals and turn the wheel. The ghosts sat above him, arguing about the best way to get to Monica's house. They nearly ran over a fat, warty toad, but there were no other mishaps – Ghost Rescue's driving was getting better.

At last they reached the address Monica had given them, and met the Clanceys. The family looked in a terrible state, pale and nervous, jumping at the slightest noise.

"They're here!" cried Monica excitedly.

"Thank you for coming," said Mr Clancey. "Goodness, Charlie, I didn't realise you were so young..."

"You're never too young to help," smiled Charlie. "Now, where's this horrible hound of yours?"

Dusk was descending as Charlie and Ghost Rescue got ready to venture among the graves. Charlie looked out of the window at the gathering gloom.

Was it the wind, or had something moved down there? And then they heard it — a howl so loud that it rattled the windowpane. A howl at once sad and furious, lonely and hungry.

Charlie's blood froze. Zanzibar whimpered and hid under the sideboard. Rio fled to the top of a wardrobe. Cookie had disappeared altogether.

"That sounds like *some* hound," whispered Florence.

"Well," sighed Lady F, "I suppose we had better go out there. After you, Charlie."

"Why do I have to go first?" asked Charlie. "You're the ghosts. You've got nothing to be scared of."

"Who said anything about being scared?" sniffed Florence.

"I don't mind going first," said Yatterdee. But then there came another howl, more awful than the first. "Hmm, on second thoughts…"

In the end they drew ghostly straws to see who would lead the way. Charlie lost.

"Typical!" he muttered. "Oh well, here I go – and I want you to follow *close behind me*! OK?"

"OK, Charlie," said four voices.

Charlie opened the door and, with the ghosts huddling behind him, he crept very slowly out into the silent graveyard.

As Charlie's eyes got used to the dark,
he could see the headstones clearly.
Some were standing upright, some
leaning at drunken angles, but all a sharp
inky black against the silver of the grass.

He looked from side to side, watching for the slightest movement – and saw it. The hound. Not moving at all, but standing there, jet black, at the far end of the graveyard.

"It's not *so* big," whispered Charlie, feeling a bit bolder. He crept closer. Still the hound made not the slightest movement, nor the faintest sound.

"Charlie…" said Lord F.

"It's all right," said Charlie. He crept even closer. "Good boy!" he said, trying to sound calm and confident. "There's a good boy!" He reached out. The hound was as still as stone.

"Charlie…" said all the ghosts at once, in a strange tone of voice.

Charlie touched the hound, expecting his hand to pass through its ghostly body. But his fingers met cold, hard stone. "*What?*" he wondered.

And then he saw the writing on its stony skin, and suddenly realised…

"It's the *headstone*! In the shape of a dog. But if that's the headstone…"

"*Charlie*…"

"…where's the *real* hound?"

"*Charlie!*"

"What is it? What—"

The growl was right behind him. It was not so much loud as *huge*.

Charlie's very bones trembled. If the growling throat was right behind his head, *how big did that make the hound?*

Charlie was frozen. He tried to turn his head, but his muscles wouldn't obey his thoughts. He imagined jaws foaming with spit, teeth as sharp as spearheads, the hound lunging to bite his head off...

Then something passed *through* him —
something huge and evil, both ice-cold
and hell-hot at the same time.

The creature landed in front of him. It
was as big as a pony. Then it turned,
slowly. Its huge body turned. Its great
head turned. And Charlie saw the *eyes* —
red fires of hatred, burning into his mind.

"*Aaaaahhh!*" Suddenly Charlie could move. He spun round, slipped on the damp grass, smashed his hip against a headstone, and ran. He ran with the Fairfaxes and Yatterdee back to the house, back to light and warmth. The hound didn't follow. It just sat back and howled a howl to make the stars shiver in the heavens.

They hid in the house until they all felt a little braver. Then they ventured out again. There was no sign or sound of the hound, and they plucked up the courage to take a closer look at the creature's headstone.

HERE LIES
BRAVEHEART
FAITHFUL FRIEND FOREVER
TO HIS MASTER BILLY BONES

"Look!" said Monica. "There's Billy Bones's grave."

"It's right next to Braveheart's grave," said Charlie. "Dog and master, together in death, as in life."

"But where," said Monica, "is Billy Bones's ghost? Why doesn't he do something to control his pet?"

"Braveheart…" said Yatterdee. "Billy Bones… I know those names… Of course! I gave Billy Bones the same tattoo twice…

"Billy was a sailor, and every time he went to sea, poor Braveheart sat on the docks awaiting his master.

"How Braveheart barked and wagged his tail when Billy's ship returned! So Billy came to me to get 'Braveheart' tattooed on one arm. But later Billy lost that arm, bitten off by a shark. So he came back to me to get 'Braveheart' tattooed on his *other* arm.

"'Yatterdee,' Billy said to me, 'I think I should get a refund on the first tattoo!'

"Yes, Billy was a cheeky fellow, brave and bold — which makes it strange that he's hiding away somewhere. I'm going to take a closer look…"

Yatterdee sank down through the ground to look at Billy's coffin. There it was, with "Billy Bones" engraved on the nameplate. Then Yatterdee poked his head inside the coffin, to look at the skeleton within…

He came rushing back to the surface. "Charlie!" he exclaimed. "Remember Billy lost an arm to the shark? Well, this skeleton has *two* arms. It isn't Billy Bones at all!"

Just then a savage snarl shook the
graveyard. There was Braveheart, huge
and terrible, with those awful fiery eyes.
The hound charged at them and leapt. As
they all tried to duck and dodge out of
the way, it flew straight through them,
and kept on running, towards...

"Cookie!" screamed Monica. "Look out!"

Cookie took one look, screeched, and bolted up a tall yew tree. Zanzibar followed, but was left whimpering at the foot of the tree, unable to climb it. As Braveheart came charging towards them, Rio seized him in his claws and struggled to haul him up into the branches. There the three animals cowered above the gnashing jaws.

Charlie, Monica and the Fairfaxes were wondering whether to run away or to try to help the animals. But Yatterdee was looking thoughtfully at the tall tree.

"I wonder..." he said. "If this isn't Billy Bones buried here, but somebody else, and if that somebody is scared of Braveheart...where would he go? *Up?*"

Yatterdee looked up, and saw the church tower on the other side of the graveyard.

"Charlie," he said, "I've got an idea. Take my stone, and throw it up into the tower."

"You want me to do *what?*" said Charlie.

"Just do it! Take good aim, and throw!"

"You've gone mad," muttered Charlie. But he got Yatterdee's stone out of his bag and weighed it in his hand. He took careful aim at a large window that might once have been glass but was now an empty hole, and hurled with all his strength.

The stone flew up, and Yatterdee flew up with it. "*Wheeeee!*"

"Good shot!" said Monica. Stone and ghost flew through the window and vanished. There was silence.

"What *is* that crazy tattooist doing?" asked Lord F.

Then Yatterdee appeared at the window.

"Hey! I've found him! Come up, quick!"

Charlie and the Fairfaxes hurried up to the top of the tower and found Yatterdee with the ghost of a man cowering in the corner.

"It's that awful beast!" moaned the ghost. "Ever since he was buried beside me, his phantom has tormented me. *Ohhhh*, will I ever be free of him?"

"It's OK," said Charlie. "We're here to help. We know you're not Billy Bones — but who are you?"

"My name is Will Jones," said the ghost. "I was buried in the wrong grave... Billy Bones and I died on the same day.

"Our two coffins lay side by side in the same funeral parlour. The undertaker was about to screw a nameplate to each coffin – 'Will Jones' to mine, 'Billy Bones' to his – when Braveheart, who was still very much alive, growled and snapped and refused to let the undertaker near his master.

"The undertaker had to lure him away with food and lock him in another room.

"At last he was able to screw on the nameplates. But with all the worry of dealing with the hound, he forgot which coffin was which. The wrong names were fixed to the coffins, and I was buried in Billy's rightful grave, and he in mine."

"Where is your rightful grave?" asked Yatterdee.

"In the graveyard at the other end of town," said Will.

"So while Will Jones haunts *this* graveyard…" said Monica.

"…Billy Bones must be haunting the *other* yard," said Charlie. "And wondering what happened to his dog!"

Later that night, the Ghostmobile
drove to the other end of town. Charlie,
Monica and the ghosts crept out into the
graveyard.

"Billy?" they called. "Billy Bones? Are
you there?"

Billy appeared, looking very surprised. "Hello!" he said. "You're the first people ever to call me by the right name. How did you know?"

They explained everything to him, and Billy was thrilled at the thought of being reunited with his hound.

"Oh, Braveheart!" he cried. "How I've missed him! How I've missed his friendly face, his kind heart, his beautiful eyes…"

"Friendly face?" said Lady F.

"Kind heart?" said Florence.

"Beautiful eyes?" exclaimed Monica.

"Er..." said Charlie, trying not to hurt Billy's feelings, "...yes, that's *definitely* your dog. And I think I know how we can get the two of you back together."

Charlie and Monica had taken a pick and a shovel from the garden shed, and now they got to work, digging up Billy's coffin. It was horrible – filthy, sweaty and tiring. But they kept at it, digging and scraping, until they were able to haul the coffin up and heave it into the back of the Ghostmobile.

"Half the job done!" said Charlie,
trying not to look as shattered as he
really was.

"Don't remind me," groaned Monica,
scraping mud from her jeans.

They drove Billy's coffin to its rightful graveyard, and of course Billy's ghost went with them. Then they dug up Will's coffin, buried Billy in his place, and finally drove back to the other end of town to bury Will in *his* rightful place. At last everyone was buried where they should be. *Phew!*

At the sight of his master, Braveheart turned at once from a howling hellhound into a playful puppy dog. The red fire faded from his eyes, his foaming snarl turned into a cheerful bark, and for the first time his great tail actually wagged with delight. He charged at Billy, leapt at him, and pinned him to the ground, licking his face.

"Good boy!" laughed Billy. "Oh,
Braveheart, did you miss me? Did you?
Did you? Who's a good boy, then?" Billy
looked at Charlie, Monica, Yatterdee and
Ghost Rescue. "Has Braveheart been a
good boy?"

They all looked at each other – and
burst out laughing.

"He's been no trouble at all, Billy," said
Charlie, crying with laughter. "No trouble
at all!"

"You know what?" said Yatterdee. "I'm going to stay behind with my old mate Billy. I miss the graveyard shift after all!"

"Well, if you need anything, you know who to call!" smiled Charlie, as they all waved goodbye from the Ghostmobile.

Ghost Rescue

WRITTEN BY
Andrew Murray

ILLUSTRATED BY
Sarah Horne

All priced at £3.99

The Ghost Rescue books are available from all good bookshops,
or can be ordered direct from the publisher:
Orchard Books, PO BOX 29, Douglas IM99 1BQ
Credit card orders please telephone 01624 836000
or fax 01624 837033 or visit our website: www.orchardbooks.co.uk
or email: bookshop@enterprise.net for details.

To order please quote title, author and ISBN
and your full name and address.
Cheques and postal orders should be made payable to 'Bookpost plc'.
Postage and packing is FREE within the UK
(overseas customers should add £1.00 per book).

Prices and availability are subject to change.